GEORGE AND MARTHA ROUND AND ROUND

For My Mother

The stories in this book were originally published by Houghton Mifflin
Company in *George and Martha Round and Round*.
Copyright © 1988 by James Marshall
Copyright © renewed 2000 by Sheldon Fogelman

www.houghtonmifflinbooks.com

Library of Congress Cataloging-in-Publication Data

Marshall, James, 1942-1992.
George and Martha : round and round / written and illustrated by James
Marshall.
p. cm.
Three of the stories that were originally published in George and Martha :
round and round, 1988.
Summary: Three stories chronicle the ups and downs of a special friendship
between two hippopotamuses.
ISBN-13: 978-0-618-98505-0
[1. Friendship–Fiction. 2. Hippopotamus–Fiction.] I. Title.
PZ7.M35672Gef 2008
[E]–dc22
2007025742

TWP 10 9 8 7 6 5 4 3 2 1
Printed in Singapore

GEORGE AND MARTHA ROUND AND ROUND

written and illustrated by
JAMES MARSHALL

HOUGHTON MIFFLIN COMPANY BOSTON

THREE STORIES ABOUT THE BEST OF FRIENDS

STORY NUMBER ONE

THE CLOCK

George gave Martha a present
for her birthday.

"It's a cuckoo clock," said George.

"So I see," said Martha.

"It's nice and loud," said George.

"So I hear," said Martha.

"Do you like it?" asked George.

"Oh yes indeed," said Martha.

But to tell the truth,
the cuckoo clock got on Martha's nerves.

The next day
George went to Martha's house.
Martha was not at home.
And the cuckoo clock
was not on the wall.
"Maybe she likes it so much
she took it with her," said George.
Just then he heard a faint
"Cuckoo . . . cuckoo . . . cuckoo."
To George's surprise,
the cuckoo clock was at the bottom
of Martha's laundry basket.

When Martha returned,
she couldn't look George in the eye.
"It must have fallen in by mistake,"
she said. "I do hope it isn't broken."
"Not at all," said George.
"The paint isn't even chipped,
the clock works just dandy,
and the cuckoo hasn't lost
its splendid voice."

"Would you like to borrow it?"
asked Martha.
George was delighted.
He found just the right spot for it, too.
Wasn't that considerate of Martha
to lend me her clock? thought George.
"Cuckoo," said the clock.

STORY NUMBER TWO

THE TRIP

George invited Martha

on an ocean cruise.

"Is *this* the boat?" said Martha.

"Use your imagination," said George.

"I'll try," said Martha.

Very soon it was raining cats and dogs.

"This is unpleasant," said Martha.

"Use your imagination," said George.

"Think of it as a thrilling storm at sea."

"I'll try," said Martha.

"Lunch is served," said George.

And he gave Martha a soggy cracker.

Martha was not impressed.

"Use your imagination," said George.

"Oh looky," said Martha.

"What a pretty shark."

"A shark!" cried George.

George took a spill.

"But where's the shark?" he said.

"Really," said Martha. "You must learn to use your imagination."

STORY NUMBER
THREE

THE ARTIST

George was painting in oils.

"That ocean doesn't look right," said Martha.

"Add some more blue.

And that sand looks all wrong.

Add a bit more yellow."

"Please," said George.

"Artists don't like interference."

But Martha just couldn't help herself.

"Those palm trees look funny," she said.

"That does it!" said George.

"See if you can do better!"

And he went off in a huff.

"My, my," said Martha.

"Some artists are *so* touchy."

And she began to make

a few little improvements.

When George returned
Martha proudly displayed the painting.
George was flabbergasted.
"You've ruined it!" he cried.
"I'm sorry you feel that way," said Martha.
"I like it."
Martha was one of those artists
who aren't a bit touchy.

JAMES MARSHALL (1942–1992)
is one of the most popular and celebrated
artists in the field of children's literature.
Three of his books were selected as New
York Times Best Illustrated Books, and he
received a Caldecott Honor Award in 1989
for *Goldilocks and the Three Bears*. With more
than seventy-five books to his credit, includ-
ing the popular George and Martha series,
Marshall has earned the admiration and
love of countless readers.